P9-DCD-601

Ruby

Alison Lester

For Edwin

Houghton Mifflin Company
Boston 1988

Library of Congress Cataloging-in-Publication Data

Lester, Alison.
Ruby.

Summary: Ruby's blanket takes her on a night flight to an island where she performs an act of great bravery.
[1. Blankets – Fiction] I. Title.
PZ7.L56284Ru 1988 [E] 87-16997
ISBN 0-395-46477-3

Published in the United States by Houghton Mifflin Company in 1988
Originally published in Australia in 1987 by Oxford University Press

Printed in Hong Kong

10 9 8 7 6 5 4 3 2 1

The Author would like to thank Rita Scharf of Oxford University Press for her faith, guidance and friendship.

When Ruby was a baby her mother made a beautiful patchwork quilt to keep her safe and warm.

As Ruby grew older, she loved her quilt more and more. She called it Besty because it was her best friend. Besty went everywhere with Ruby.

Besty always lay on Ruby's bed as she slept. With Besty on her bed Ruby could sleep safely through the night, protected from the serpent she was sure lived under her bed.

But one hot summer night Ruby went to bed without Besty. Her mother had washed Besty that day and it was still out on the clothesline.

Ruby thought she couldn't live through the night without Besty. She climbed out the window to fetch Besty, making sure she kept far away from the serpent.

Softly she padded across the dry lawn.

Besty seemed to beckon Ruby from the clothesline.

As Ruby grasped Besty's corners, she felt herself rising gently into the night air.

Silently she rose above the houses and trees.

Ruby was flying!

Higher and faster she flew up over the bay,
leaving behind the lights of the sleeping city.

MAGIC CARPET
AIRLINES
CATS
RUBY
RED
BEST
BLANKETS
King Leo
Wine

The stars were very close and the sea shimmered silver as Ruby rode Besty.

In the distance Ruby saw an island.

Besty and Ruby glided down on to the island beach.

There some animals were waving anxiously.

'We need your help!' cried Queen Zinnia. 'Our cubs have been kidnapped by the vicious serpent Sarazin. Today is the triplets' birthday, and we have prepared a midnight feast. But Sarazin has cast a terrible spell.'

Ruby followed the tearful family down to the river. There she saw the miserable cubs huddled on the opposite bank. Coiled in a tree was the vicious serpent Sarazin, its eyes glistening with cruel pleasure.

‘Even my husband King Vidor and our loyal equerry Sir Uncle Elmo are powerless,’ sobbed Queen Zinnia. ‘Only you and Besty can save our children.’ Ruby felt her heart grow cold.

Ruby flung Besty over her shoulders and edged out on to the mossy log. She was shaking a little, but raised her head to stare fiercely at Sarazin. The serpent slithered back into the jungle.

Ruby gathered the tear-stained cubs into her arms.

Proudly she carried the babies back across the river. Queen Zinnia, King Vidor and Sir Uncle Elmo were overcome with joy.

Now the birthday celebrations could begin.

‘You have saved our beloved children and we grant you and Besty the freedom of our country,’ boomed King Vidor in his deep growly voice. ‘You are welcome here forever.’

The cubs performed their tumbling act in honour of Ruby and Besty.

And Queen Zinnia presented Ruby with the highest honour of the land — the Blue Bird of Bravery. Sir Uncle Elmo sewed the medallion on to Besty with gold thread.

The sky was growing pale in the east. It was time for Ruby and Besty to go home.

Besty carried Ruby up and away. Behind her Ruby could hear the sound of Sir Uncle Elmo's lute as the birthday revels went on.

Soon Ruby was back in bed fast asleep.

When she woke the sun was high in the sky. Ruby looked at Besty lying in the usual place on her bed. The Blue Bird seemed to wink at her in the morning sun.

Ruby found her old overalls under the bed and got ready for breakfast.